Oblations

Nick Ripatrazone

Published by Gold Wake Press
Editor: J. Michael Wahlgren
http://goldwakepress.org

ISBN: 978-0-9826309-6-9

Cover image by Jennifer Ripatrazone

Oblations

GOLDWake Press

Boston, Ma.

Acknowledgments

Many thanks: J. M. Wahlgren's support of the project; the mentoring of Gary Fincke, Tom Bailey, Alice Elliott Dark, Rachel Hadas, Jayne Anne Phillips and Paul Lisicky; the love and generosity of my parents (Michael and Lynn) and family (Mark, Mike, and Cara); the incredible love and friendship of my wife, Jennifer.

The following poems previously appeared in publications:

Barn: Howell (*West Branch*)
Barn: Gunn (*West Branch*)
Barn: Flynn (*West Branch*)
Calvin Stone (*Beloit Fiction Journal*)
Noone Pender (*Beloit Fiction Journal*)
William Williams (*Beloit Fiction Journal*)
Montoya (*Swarthmore Literary Review*)
The Buffalo Fence (*Yale Journal for Humanities in Medicine*)
Holy Family (*Salt River Review*)
Work: Fishing (*Terrain: A Journal of the Built and Natural Environments*)
Work: Gardening (*Terrain: A Journal of the Built and Natural Environments*)
Work: Herding (*Terrain: A Journal of the Built and Natural Environments*)
Work: Landscaping (*Terrain: A Journal of the Built and Natural Environments*)
Work: Milling (*Terrain: A Journal of the Built and Natural Environments*)

Table of Contents

Oblations

All things counter, original, spare, strange. --Gerard Manley Hopkins

The first three:

A maculated dog, black melding into brown, each ovate spot patched and pale.

Raddled bougainvillea creeping over enamel-white curb.

Salmonberry and oxtongue leaning forward from the shore of a sallow farm pond, striae forming along the mud wall.

Beauty in the dappled and pied.

I
Barns

Barn: Howell

Auburn clapboard. Rafters paled from swallows. New roof, 1978.

Susan and Helen Howell, sisters.

Married blond men from Boise but kept their maiden name. Mother always said that was her wish. Her hands were always cold, even after minutes in front of the gas range, hours under blankets. Susan's husband twisted his ankle on a loose floorboard and cursed God. Susan told him to relax and tried to take off his boot but he pushed her backward. The four of them--Susan, Helen, and the two husbands--stood there, silent, awaiting guidance, as if it would swell like wind through the open loft door. Mother was dead by then. The cows were sick, heads slogging along the sodden grass. No one knew what should happen next.

Barn: Coburn

Box-frame. Holstein farm from 1945 to 1981.

Patricia and Dan Coburn, couple.

Patricia still dreamed about the red and whites until 1989, when her son
left for college. Dan supported his son's interest in Pomona. He'd driven
the hatchback there, the ride home interrupted by heavy, heaving rain that
clubbed the roof, drops snapping like rocks. They pulled the hatchback
under an overhang and waited. Palmed peanuts bought from the rest stop.
And waited. Patricia said it was a sign. She repeated that with confidence
the entire ride home, then left Dan alone in the house and went to the barn.
She remembered the cows herringboned there. The parlor had lain
untouched for all these years. So many promises had been made: promises
of love, promises of work. Declarations of what was next. But those cows
were gone, and that parlor was bare. All things only needed time to
disappoint.

Barn: Gunn

Barrel vault. North end woodpecked.

Dale Gunn.

Retired from Forest Service in 1983 after 32 years, most spent in towers. Caught sight of the May 1978 blaze that sucked the southern slope of Hacklebarney. Stored two tractors in the barn. Both bought at estate sales. Went to the estate sales with the same goal: to find newspaper clippings of college basketball games. His nephew was a collector. It was a gift he could count on; something that could be repeated each year. Knew that many people piled newspapers in garages, barns, foot-deep in grass. Found both tractors the same weekend, both Massey Fergusons. Brought them to the barn on a low trailer and, once retired, planned to put them to work. Opened the barn doors, stood in front of the silent machines. Considered things. Closed the barn doors and called a mechanic.

Barn: Frank

Double-gambrel. True red.

Sharon and Samuel Frank, couple.

Bottom row of windows shattered in February 1991. Sharon found the damage after work and went inside. Shards patterned across the floor but she couldn't find stones, baseballs, or bullets. Samuel thought it had been done with a hammer. Pointed to footprints in the snow. Sharon assured him they were from deer. Ate scrambled eggs for dinner with a healthy amount of bacon. Too much bacon, they both agreed afterward. Samuel went into the attic, came down with his Winchester, and almost reached the back door when Sharon asked what he was doing. Said there was another row of windows left, that they'd be back. He pulled the deerstalker over his head and sat on a folding chair in the snow. He lasted for 15 minutes before coming inside, face flushed, and blamed it all on the deer.

Barn: Flynn

Round. Mow hold: 35 tons, loose.

David and Payton Flynn, brothers.

Windrows curled along the soft hills. Payton was older. David was taller. Payton wanted to spread the manure in March. Said there was no more snow; said there would be no more frost. David said the runoff would sour the soil but he was never very forward for a man of his height. David was correct and used that fact to barter his way through a thousand decisions: new tractor, new pickup, even choices of women. Payton had a soft spot for brunettes with light eyes. Called them God's mistakes. David said that he needed to test each woman out, sit with her, have a drink (both whiskey and coffee), see how long her attention spanned. David said he was only doing it for Payton's own good. Then he fell in love with one of Payton's girls and was afraid to tell him. Instead watched his brother lead the team of Appaloosas into the stable and hoped he would just disappear there. Wished he'd been wrong about that runoff.

Barn: Mattson

Stairs to the loft. Roof brighter than the Tennessee bluegrass matted along the base.

Erin Mattson

Brothers and father built the barn during the summer of 1984. They lived in Plainview and made the hour drive each morning and night. One brother got angry and said he'd sleep in the barn and he did, unfinished roof open to the stars. That same brother got caught watching *Metti una Sera a Cena* in the basement when he was 15 and that fact became a way to silence him in all conversations. But they did not invoke the film that night. Thought it was better to let him drift under the air. He woke with a sore throat and Erin gave him a long hug, through the planers scraping along timber and the boots climbing the bright roof. She had plans for three quarter horses. She had so many plans. She kept lists on the kitchen table and sometimes her notes pushed through the soft pine. She pulled her fingers along the indentations for months afterward, reminded of her intentions. Then she put a tablecloth over the wood and forgot.

Barn: Thayer

Chestnut. Breech beams. White cross on back siding.

Tracy and Bill Thayer, couple.

Tracy was Lutheran, Bill was Catholic, but both turned their eyes at the cross painted along the pine siding. The Army Corps of Engineers marked property borders with those white crosses. County register supported the claim; clerk wondered how they couldn't have noticed the boundaries when they purchased the property. Tracy said sometimes things are missed. Bill didn't think it a big deal. Thought about staining it chestnut but Tracy wouldn't let him. She walked, double-gloved, through the woods to find the next property. Brought a canteen and flashlight. Came back at dusk; Bill, on the porch, wore a told-you-so look. She never told him what she'd found. But she did let him stain away the cross.

Barn: Dowd

Parts hand hewn. Butternut? Probably black walnut.

Anne and Lawrence Dowd, couple.

Lawrence had an adze but he couldn't hew. Stared at the barn for long minutes and said the roof had an uneven slope. Anne told him to stop staring at the barn; people would think him crazy. He said they were in the house alone; who else would notice? She thought her own opinion of him was enough. She had lavish dreams about balls in that barn. Wondered if such a thing ever happened. Dreamt she danced with a blond man. She stared into the rafters and saw Lawrence crying, sitting on a bale. His tears did not bother her. Not during the dream, not afterward. She never much liked blond men before that dream but did afterward. Thought she should, having dreamt about one. Had no interest in other men, though, but did wonder if Lawrence could be blond. He was brown through and through: eyes, hair, even skin a bit dark. So she was stuck: this dream, this reality, this husband who stares and stares.

Barn: Larson

Loshoe: wide doorway, double. Pigs through at sunrise, back at sunset.

Eli Larson

Near the hearth was the "1831 Room": wallpapered blue and white, cherry table and chairs, orange-glass lamp. Half-sofa under the window. Eli sometimes slept there: usually after nights of bourbon and chicken at the Hamp-Towne Pub, three miles up county road 515. His brother Travis would bring him home, shift Eli over a shoulder (Eli was 155, Travis 215: they did share the same color eyes), unlatch the door opposite the gable, then carry him upstairs to the sofa. Eli never learned; or rather, didn't care that he'd end-up face down on the pub counter. He expected Travis to save him in that manner. To bring him to that room so he could wake with the gray sky on his face (his bed in the house was in clear sight of the sun; the barn bordered by willows). But one night Travis decided otherwise. There was no direct reason; no argument, no bad day at work. Sometimes decisions are merely accumulated, released emotion. Eli woke leaning against the back of the pub. But the sky was still gray there.

Barn: McDonaghue

Forebay: kept snow from stable doors. Log and frame.

Jason and Hannah McDonaghue, couple.

Adopted a child from California. Told people it was a "long story," but it really was not: Jason served in Vietnam with a Palo Alto man, whose wife left for Mexico a week after their baby was born. The man wasn't about to raise a girl on his own. Jason took the child. Hannah was fine with that: her mother had told her stories of childbirth, of veined stomachs and vomit, of cravings for sex and sardines, of hatred and love in equal parts. The child loved onion and potato pirogues, asked for plate after plate, covered in pepper. Knew she was adopted. Knew that her father had a tattoo of an eagle across his back. That the eagle had red eyes. Loved living in Sioux Falls, though, as she aged, knew it was difficult to understand if another place was better if a person only knew one. Stood under the forebay as the snow fell and piled at her back and wondered: did her mother speak English in Mexico? If she didn't, and she met her mother, how would they speak? Are words really necessary?

Barn: Pierce

Wall-vents for airing broadleaf tobacco had become stuffed with swallow thistle.

Marian Pierce.

Father told her no man was worth dying for, and she didn't understand the comment at the moment. She was seventeen, a good field hockey player, a better liar: not to her father, who was worthy of the truth, but to boys in the back of station wagons, behind restaurants, and once, under the carport of her third cousin's best friend. She would do nothing beyond kiss. And even that felt like too much, until one night, after closing her mouth, she swore she would keep it closed for good. The boy had asked how she planned on eating. She walked home, most of the way along the center yellow line, hopping forward to land on the paint when it became dashed. That was when her father gave the advice. At first she thought he'd misunderstood. But the next morning, as he walked out to the flapping sheets above the tobacco, his words made perfect sense. She repeated them aloud, lips close to the curtains.

Barn: Davidson

House-and-carriage. Fieldstone, from northern county quarry.

Benjamin and Tanya, Karen, Gustave, Connor, Particia Yolen, family.

Boys on one side, girls on the other side of the table. Fruitwood, drawer on the boys' side (discovered there one Sunday afternoon: balled, undercooked pancake in a napkin). Connor never kept his hands on the table, always on his thighs, wool pants he wanted to wear in all weather (he'd watched a bicentennial recreation in Highstate Park). Gustave was older, though not any wiser: that title went to Karen, who had returned home from Bates with all the knowledge one could hope about James Frazer. Calling the loaves and the fishes a myth, she explained, did not to devalue their Methodist faith she still shared. Patricia just nodded her head: the week before she'd seen her parents--for the first time in her memory--kissing behind the barn like teenagers. But the barn was connected to the house, so it was only a matter of time before their love moved inside.

II
Baseball

Barrett Stickle

Switched after a year from pitcher to coach. Scouted; sometimes three games a day. People asked if he dreamt about baseball but he said no; he dreamt about sleeping. Found three long-leggers from Duluth, rode the rain with them back to Chicago. The three were not much for talking, though he tried his best. Always thought he was meant to teach the game rather than play. Explained most things in analogies to sex. Kept those explanations clean because he was Lutheran. Somehow he managed. Realized that vagueness kept him safe in life. Worked primarily with southpaws. Felt they could best see the part of the field that mattered most. Had tried to pitch lefty himself and became embarrassed after the first throw. Vowed to never again try such a thing in public. Yet remained tied to his love of all things left in secret. Kissed his wife on that cheek. Held that hand. Wrote, ate, shaved left. Felt that life was worth nothing if you could not grow into such a decision. Thought it unfair that we are assigned a role in this existence, least of all those of body. Tried to raise his son a lefty. At first only when his wife wasn't looking, but then all of the time. The boy did gravitate toward that hand but his wife said it was either because Barrett had tricked him into the choice or that the boy's movements were natural and Barrett's efforts were a waste. He ignored her and brought the boy to Navin Field. They watched Dutch Leonard but never spoke a word about hands.

Box Joseph

5 foot 5. 202. Triceps like flanks. Dockworker. Walked out of school after the first grade. Catcher. Threw from the crouch. Pants tight at the quads. Scrambled eggs for lunch and dinner. Slept in his uniform before games on the road. Smoked High Admirals and dipped Copenhagen. Drank brandy with milk, the mix a thin brown. Knocked an in-the-park home run the night Babe Ruth hit his first. Had a son. Said it was with one woman and then with another. His mother sat him down with the pastor and they made a list. Anna, Teresa, Gwendolyn, Sarah, Terri. Definitely not Terri, he said, and leaned back. They decided on Anna and he went to her house with roses and pound cake. Her boyfriend opened the door and stood face to face with Box, with that strength of knowing that he stood in his own home. Box set the roses and cake on the front porch and left. A week later Anna left the boy on Box's front porch. His mother watched the boy and named him Jude. She chose the name. Eyes some days blue and others green. She changed his clothes on a washboard. Mashed peaches with a pork and drained the juice. Box stuffed gauze in his mitt. Constant back problems. Took baths with primrose, sweet violet, and willow bark. Slept on a bare bed, slept on springs. One game he fell forward onto home plate in the midst of a batter's swing. The bat missed his head by the width of a leaf. Walked the rest of his life with a cane. When his mother died he took the boy back home. He was only 6. The boy brought him walking sticks from the woods. Pine and oak. Pared them down with a knife, smoothed them with sandpaper. Held his father's hand as they walked down the street. The boy picked up a bat when he was 8. It felt good in his hands. Box said his swing was crisp. There really is nothing like that snap.

Calvin Stone

Left-handed pitcher. Slow leg on the mound. No one ever knew his true height because he always slumped, shoulders hunched, eyes turned to home plate. Short fingers. For a pitcher, for a man. Dipped his fingertips in molasses and two bits water before games. Gave his pitches a certain wobble. Practiced from a mound double the distance. Wanted the ball to reach home mid-speed, mid-spin. Hated when pitches dipped and dove. Sister gave him a recipe for banana cake but he made cornmeal pie. Flat, pressed, golden: almost black. He never had a taste for fruit. Wore his tendons thin: popped out his shoulder during dinner while reaching across the table for butter. Shoulder stayed in a shrug the entire night. Wife wrapped a bedsheet around his arm and pulled. Always a good feeling, that relaxing of skin, the return to shape. Slept with ice in a pillowcase. Woke with a puddle on the sheets, in the mattress. Once it dripped onto his dress shoes below, paling the leather. Struck out seven in a row on a Saturday, all on the same 2-1 set, and then walked the next run home, feeling that good fortune came in discernable waves. Traded for Dale Curtis and a tractor. An Allis-Chalmers. Calvin lost each game that season. 0-11. Never a close score, always at least double the runs. Dale had a 1.36 ERA. Lived and died by the spit. Kept the ball tucked to his stomach through the windup. Calvin watched him one night in Cleveland and quit baseball the next day. Became a park ranger in southern Kentucky. The tractor lived on for years. It was even fitted with a harrow that chucked hay into the slow Missouri wind. The owner took it down a rocky pitch one winter and it never ran the same again. Sat to rot in an unused stable, next to an Appaloosa fitted with a cribbing collar.

Ennis Cole

Corn Creek Gun Club. Half a mile off county road 622. Enough signs to find it if you knew what could be found. Photographs of rabbits hung in the basement, held by roofing nails from the double-paneling. Father's father was a member. Father was a member and was giving a class when rifle repeated and shot himself dead in front of the chalkboard. For half a minute nobody moved. Membership passed down to Ennis, who was loose with a gun. Had an elbow twitch that he'd spent years calming down to a metered tic. He swung early to compensate, to take back control. He stuffed down the gun club dinners, elbows wide on the table. Someone left a note in his locker: you can't shoot like your father. Which was fine.

Erickson Wyatt

Long arms, stood far from the plate. Heel of his hand against the knob. Clean swing: smooth crack from shoulder to shoulder. Practiced over a chair, a trash can. Thought about sitting his brother on a stool and swinging above his hair but there was no need for such risk in sport, business, or love. Liked to be set in things, content. Married his first girlfriend. They had met in grammar school. Asked later if "meet" was something that could happen so young; he said her eyes hadn't changed, so yes. They rented a two-room on the south side though they could have done better. He had three good seasons in a row--at bat and on the field. Played lacrosse before he picked up a glove so he had a fine sense of length. Could eye a foot, a yard, even a quarter mile. Did everything by sight. No need for a ruler. Learned that if he was correct once or twice then accuracy would be assumed. Had a bad season--bobbled grounders, swung too early--and was more surprised than he should have been. So he sat out the next season. Wife had to leave the children with him at home. He had no idea what to do. He hadn't watched her, hadn't learned. Thought he'd never have the need. They ran the house while he sat at the sink, ice cubes pushed against his cheeks with his tongue. It was the only way he could cool down. Wife taught at the grammar school. Knew that her soft voice was a blessing in the classroom: it meant that students had to listen closely to hear her words. She told them that these early years were the most important of their lives; commitments and promises made now would remain with them until their final days.

Gray Whitney

Hair paled white at 13. It happened during the summer and they called him a ghost. He always swung early: pulled the ball down the 3rd base line. He played in 5 games in 1891. That was all. His long arms enabled him to hold the end of the bat when he bunted. He practiced with a soaked ball, reading the slog and wobble in the air. He stole something when he was 7 and his father scolded him. Gray could hear him from down the street. Except his name was not yet Gray: it was Thomas. The yell was so deep there was no way to look at his father the same afterward, as if his skin had been scorched by the sound. His father came to a Washington game, the last of the year. He ate a turkey sandwich. His hands were a wet mess and he wiped them along his peacoat. The stains shined, even in dusk. They had dinner together and it was the longest they'd ever spoken. They were always interrupting each other. Not to finish each other's sentences but to break into them. His father had roast mallard and currant, and three glasses of port, side-by-side, at once. His father went to the bathroom and left without coming back. Gray paid for the dinner with his last dollars and snuck on the St. Louis train, closed his coat around his face and snored. His throat wobbled from the sound. When he woke the conductor was sitting next to him, reading *Vick's Monthly*. Gray became the 3rd base coach for the Cubs. He always loved that part of the field. Until a line-drive smashed him on the chin in 1914. He wore the stitches like a beard. For a few games he stood at his side, chest facing the outfield. Claimed he could still see home plate. They released him when two straight players were thrown out trying to steal home. For three years he taught near-sighted children to hit. He hung a tennis ball from a branch. One morning he found the tennis ball gone, the string frayed. He took the train somewhere, and wherever that was, he remained.

King Dolan

Father was the sheriff of Essex County, New York. Took a rifle shot in the knee: from a carbine, he guessed. Swore he saw the tip pull back into brush. King found him on the sidewalk, hand on thigh. Hand should have been on his knee. Pointed to the brush and King followed the trail of his finger. Found nothing: trust that he would have found something if something could be found. Later his father's hand moved inside a woman's thin blouse while she sat on his desk. Got a small-town second-chance but lost his position. Became a deputy. Then King found the blouse, hung alone in a bureau. A silk, beige trophy. Thought about that, about blouses and hands, while tucked away in left-field. In St. Louis, in Cleveland, and once in Kansas City. King lost everything in the sun: liners, pop-ups, bouncers. The same was true off the field: he'd be walking with his wife and catch glance of a hawk and could see nothing more. The wings became tight and then all was gone. He couldn't even see the hand she waved inches from his nose. Though he could feel it. He paid attention to hands. Palms is the better word. He paid attention to palms and didn't care for the back of hands. Called King because he always sat at the head of the table. As a boy, as a man. Once the manager took them to dinner after the pennant and King sat front and center. The manager didn't say a word. Sometimes power is passed with a whimper or a smile.

Lehn Wallace

His wife was tall. Raised on a strawberry farm and took to a boy's chores: raked the green berries into an overturned can, swept pebbles from the carport, stained the worm fence. Had a permanent brown-black dye beneath her fingers, so that when Lehn's mother helped her wash sweet potatoes for the wedding dinner she led Ellen to the table and held the hands between her knees and scrubbed with a tight wire brush. Dipped her skin in water filled with lemon, chamomile, rind. Ellen merely nodded. The wedding was long. At one point everyone paused, turned in the pews, and wondered why they were still there. Even the priest looked bored. Lehn had a game the next day and followed the caravan with his wife and rested her hand on his crotch. She was bad. Three boyfriends a month type. Tongues along gums during the first kiss. The type who would lean over the center field wall to snag a triple and leave her hands there to be touched. Lehn played second and was a good fielder but asked to be switched to the outfield. At first the coach thought him a fool but he brought Ellen to practice and said this, this is what makes me nervous. After the switch he kept an eye on her and sometimes men sat near. He would ask her after the game: why didn't you move? She would say that she liked her seat. One late afternoon game he dropped a slow fly and blamed it on her. Said he could see a man's arm around her shoulders. She took the car home and left him at the field. He called his mother and she picked him up in a Model T. She pulled up slowly and he stepped back on the curb. He felt the need to keep moving: to avoid being still. She got out of the car when he got in and said, where is she? He waved his mother back. Said she always knew Ellen was bad. Her fingers could never be cleaned. You need to see in front of your eyes, Lehn, she said. But it was hard for him to see because of the wind.

Noone Pender

Beaned on the elbow his first at-bat. Cockeyed swing afterward. Bad handshake. Scratchy signature. Team doctor told him to start with a coffee cup, filled, held straight at arm's length. Black or lightened with milk? Didn't matter. Then tried a gallon of water. His next at-bat he stood back from the plate but stepped in at the last moment. Cracked a spinner down center, rounded first, a healthy length. Game was called that inning from lightning. He always took his Grant roadster to the games. Parked at the insulation factory on Orange Street. Everybody told him not to. Coach said to park elsewhere. Players agreed. Manager promised the same, and his brother was a stockholder in the company. The roadster was stolen that night of lightning, that night of thick rain. His suit became ruined during the long walk home. Slept in his bathtub. Cradled his elbow against his chest. Twice late for practice on account of brandy: it was the only way to ease the sting. Sat the next game. That was the night of Addie Joss's perfect game. Noone would always bring up that night in conversations: conversations about baseball, duck hunting, electrical work. Conversations at the post office, after mass, on the back steps of a brothel in Washington state. When pressed for details he first stood his ground--said how Joss sweat everywhere but his teeth, said he was with him until his final days-- but always had to admit, sooner or later, that he was not playing that night. That he was on the sideline of history. That he had never seen Joss except for one night in Dodge County. A warm night in January. Men with sport coats draped over their shoulders. And Joss leaned against a savings and loan building, arms crossed, shoes crossed. Still sweating.

Parker Patterson

Played in that first college football match between Rutgers and Princeton. Played for the latter team though he dropped out of the college afterward. During the match he was knocked with a side hit and scratched his cornea. Thought it a bruise and left it untreated. Many told him it was worse than he thought but he liked to trust himself. He thought it was necessary to do that. He brought the match into conversation whenever possible and pointed to his eye. It looked like a normal eye except for a streak across the white that could have been bloodshot but never faded. Explained that the injury had nothing to do with how he could pitch. Promised his sight was straight and sure, and he did move with tight form, could make strike after strike. Though he did need to throw every day to keep his arm loose, his aim right. Others said they did the same but Parker assured them: everyday. So often we avoid the truth in declarations of time. But Parker meant what he said: pale-spotted with measles, he pitched. Or stomach soured after bad tilapia. Or when his father he died; he attended the funeral, held the mourning at his house, excused himself to the bathroom, climbed out the window, and pitched into the back of his shed, plywood leaned against the planks. Back inside mud pasted along the sides of his dress shoes but he assured them it was nothing. Even after he stopped playing--after he could barely reach home plate without the catcher having to shift--he continued to throw. There was no reason to stop. Curveballs into the trunks of willows; fastballs rising wide and shattering the glass of a barn. Pitches lost in the air forever; pitches that rolled to a rest somewhere in wheat fields. He would follow most of them and find the majority. But others remained under rain and snow.

William Williams

Bearded. Kept it close. Kept it even. But the manager still had a problem. Said only drunkards and longshoremen kept beards. And neither of them played for the Browns. After he shaved the stubble he showed pockmarks, rings of blue, thin skin. Manager said to grow the hair back. Played left field for the first 71 games, right for the final 84. Played an inning at center but felt the field too wide. Squinted beneath the sun. Squinted beneath the clouds. Took a healthy hop before each throw. Accurate to a center uniform button. Never a bounce catch, never an arm stretch. At the chest, at the heart, where a throw belongs. Went to college. Studied geology. Considered the effect of water on land. How currents tend to flatten, form curves, change the shape of original things. Spoke to the crowd during games. Never discussed baseball. Kept a letter in his back pocket. Fumbled a catch each Wednesday in March during 1911. His girlfriend Tess found meaning in all patterns: she paused before quilts of crosslets, afghans of diamonds. She counted the nodes on leaves and the rings on tree stumps. Even if the counting meant standing beneath heavy rain. She convinced William to see a diviner. In Hoboken. Near the train station. William said he couldn't believe the supernatural existed in a city. The diviner agreed. So they drove miles to Warren County, where they parked at the edge of a gravel road and walked to the center of a wheat field, where the diviner dropped William's glove in the mud. When he got it the next day it was full of owl pellets. It was a hell of a time to clean. But he never missed another ball.

Tris Hooper

Second base for the St. Louis Brown Stockings. Knock-kneed: you could hear his kneecaps smack as he ran across the wheatgrass; while he walked in trousers; while he stood at the sink for a shave. He was called: Burned, Tattle, Trick, Scooper. Teetotaller: at least until he was 38, when his sister bought him a fifth of Heaven Hill bourbon and said here, this is what you've been missing. Then he spent some weekends lying beneath an ale barrel, lips sticky like syrup, eyes wild. That was 1876. When they still pitched underhand. They did not throw. Tris was a barehanded catcher when the rest wore buckskin gloves. He washed his hands in rock salt. Tried sandpaper but his palms kept the cuts and he bled the sleeves of long shirts. Dragged his knuckles along dirt to scoop the ball. Brought up a cloud of dust that hung around his shoulder while he tossed. Once hit two triples during an overcast game. Said the ball was lost in the dark. Leaned his left hand out as he rounded the bases, back at a bend. Used a pitch pine bat, knobless. Grew up on a poultry farm in Ashland where his father taught him to kill Wyandottes but never wrung a neck until Holy Thursday, 1868, when he killed one of his mother's Rosecombs at dawn but then dropped it in the dirt and fell asleep. His brother was a haberdasher. Sold red and white ribbons in Portland. Maine, not Oregon. Only slept with women with long names: Margareth, Henrettea, Charlotte. Once broke his manager's nose. It wasn't even a good punch. Shattered his ankle during a stump match in 1891. Wobbled off the field, out the fence, down the street. Never played again. Married a woman in Carson City in 1899. Her name was short: A. She had forgotten the rest. By then he had changed his taste in most things. Postmaster of Owyhee, Nevada. Shot walking home from work in 1911. Died in the street. The next week his wife received a letter saying he would be included in the St. Louis Hall of Fame. She never even knew he played the game.

III
Miscellanea

Montoya

1.
We boarded a hostler from San Fernando. Man said he fought in two wars and wore scars on both thighs. We never asked to see; he never offered to show.

2.
He broke the horses in less time than it takes me to make an omelet. He stood on the back porch, boots unlaced, mud like a mole on his cheek.

3.
Said he had a woman in Pomona. He showed us folded sketches that creased along her thin nose. Her eyes were wide almonds. Later my husband said a lack of photographs is a lack of love.

4.
Did we see that man cry. Leaning against the paddock, a montero on his head, gloves on his hands. The sketches flamed in a ten-gallon drum, going wherever smoke goes and staying there.

Séance

Everything was on the table: *The Changing Light at Sandover*, cognac and tulip glasses, a Ouija board emblazoned with Hassan's initials in some Arabic script. He was born in Bahrain but left before he spoke his first word. I always thought that language was the test of residency: say a word, speak a world. Yet he carries the anecdote like a necklace, shined so gold it looks like brass. My eyes linger on his neck for a long moment, and he catches me, and I catch James: the three of us at a table with four chairs, mouths dry, heavy hands on thin cardboard.

Infected

My uncle said humans couldn't get Texas fever. The cattle disease. That was 1987, in Laredo. In front of the mechanic's shop. One of the mechanics cut hair in the back. In a room behind the cars. Away from the oil but you could still smell it. He wore his blue mechanic suit that only reached the tops of his boots. He washed his hands with soap heavy as a rock. My uncle said the cattle got it from ticks but for a few years nobody knew the real cause. Those must have been weird years, with that disease buzzing around, cattle plodding, bellies low in the grass, slouching over hills. We were scared of AIDS then. My uncle said there was no such thing as sure protection, so he just stopped having sex. Altogether. He envied the cattle, plodding, heads leaned forward, unaware of what could be passed.

To Luck
After W.S. Merwin

We try to explain you without understanding but sometimes description alone is enough. You've had some tiffs with coincidence, and all his flighty connections (that stubborn need to connect all things). You even called Plutarch an asshole. That was a bit much. But you are forgiven your whims; after all, that is your trait most essential. How you come and go before we know your form. We try to illustrate you through example, to trick you into revelation: we say that you are the element that allows a knock-kneed boy to cross the white finish line first in some indiscriminate Indiana school race, teachers and parents leaning over the fence, mouths agape, praising the boy but, between spoken words, thanking you.

The Toboggan Party

After 33 push-ups my triceps stung. Cal piled weights on my back: not a single stack, rather a line along my spine. With each repetition I saw his boots, brown leather bleached beige from salting. He got the plow call an hour ago, but promised to see this bet through. Old Milwaukee cans crimped and drained in the sub pump waft through the basement, so with mouth closed I reached 50 and collapsed, weights clinking, pushing me into the carpet. Cal cursed, kicked the wall and a frame rattled. A landscape with long-coated Frenchmen sliding down a steep hill.

His payment was the same number of push-ups outside in the snow. His entire body was covered--thermals and jackets, pants tucked into socks--save for his hands. He finished and stood, shaking as he walked toward the truck. Only an inch of us needs to be cold for our entire body to know the feeling.

Certain Notes of Remembrance of a Religious Service on August 7, 1755

The Scot pastor, Harold McCohn, wore a frock-shirt, sleeves draped over his hands. He shook back the fabric to turn pages of scripture. His back-tied belt was buffalo-leather; his moccasins sheepskin. His wife stood at the back of the parish, barefoot, browned heels shifting on the wood. McCohn read the fourth chapter of Job and then explained how he and his wife would spend each evening in fear of the Cree. He said that fear is a problem, of course, but worry was worse, a more constant emotion. Worry leads to imagination, and so McCohn spent every night awake, eyes open in the dark, waiting for a tap on the door to report the arrival of Cree. A dagger beneath his pillow. He paused, sighed. All ten people in the congregation attested to that breath. Such worry, he promised, will lead us nowhere. All we really need is faith.

Under the Bleachers, Halifax West HS, 1983

Tracy slept during gym while her classmates paced around the track, most with hands in pockets, one boy striding forward, yellow and blue socks pulled to his knees; Barry popped whippets while listening to Rush on a Walkman, left headphone chewed by his younger brother (the black foam curled on his small tongue); Ray and Jessica kissed but wanted more: hands here and there, backs against a dismantled fence, she remembering what her sister had said about him; Carl looked at the back of mothers' legs, jean shorts folded twice at the thigh, thinking of his father's girlfriend, the new one who works the last register at Shop Rite, curly hair black and yellow, tied back though a few strands always stuck left, limp and worn.

A. J. Cole

Spent 1980-1985 at Ralston Gate County Jail, one of the first prison horse programs. The Bureau of Land Management rounded hundreds of mixed breeds and the inmates lined the paddock wall during the first day. One horse at a time walked through the chute and chose a man.

Cole broke 45 horses during his time.

Released the day after his birthday, or what he though to be his birthday (the certificate was signed by a barber, not a doctor). Hired in northern Virginia to maintain a Lutheran cemetery, pushed a mower between the rows of forward-leaning gravestones. Careful to not let his feet cross over a heart. Fine for the mower blades to do so but not a part of him. Knew that was where he was going, sooner or later, and the least he could expect in life was some measure of reciprocation.

Nelson: Found August 1968

Face down in the Rockaway River, current rushed from morning wind.
Stomach half-full of whiskey, half-full with shepherd's pie from The Dart.
The night before he'd leaned over the counter, forearms on the wood, forks
in both hands. He scooped healthy amounts. Starving. He was very tall:
so high he slouched. He always had problems with his back, even from
youth (pediatrician walked fingers along his spine and said it was more
crooked than the mayor). Three boys found him, their long lines snapping
for trout, one wayward cast hooked on khakis. At first it felt like a big fish.
That initial identity of a catch is usually unclear.

Bugged

Nothing safe. Boll weevil: cotton field. Corn earworm: Texas. Railroad worm: burrow inside apple, flesh becomes pulped. Consider, also with apples: the San Jose scale leaves rough, brown marks. Powder-post beetle attacks doorjambs and building rafters (the Potter farm, you know, is overcome with eggs, tunneled in wood; the old man had steamed for a week and still the beige pellets dropped). Horn flies stuck on the shoulders of cattle. Bred in manure (all their lives shifting in shit). Cattle killed by screw-worm infection wound, blood dripping, almost curling. Onion thirp attacked onions. Fresh, new ones, but also those stored, discarded, or forgotten.

Flophouse, Room 107

A cross was painted along the ceiling sometime between 1976 and 1980. Tenant died. Owner stood on a chair, then a ladder, whitewashed the mark. Next tenant--a former ironworker from lower Detroit--repainted the cross. Painted it black with a purple outline. Owner had to stop by the room some December; tenant said pipes had leaked from upstairs. Hell of a thing: water must have taken a few right turns, coasted along walls, found its way there. Owner showed before noon, after lunch (sloppy joe on rye, two beers, both skunked). Tenant had peeled back a patterned circular rug: naked woman, big nipples. Pointed to the discolored wood below, said it was still moist to the touch. Owner got on his knees, pressed his palm on the floor. Looked up. Thought that cross looked better than the previous one.

The Buffalo Fence

Laotians traditionally mixed dung with beetlenut to salve a burned hand or infected foot. Such treatment was no longer necessary. We whitewashed the dispensary at Muong Sing and wrapped wire from post to post to keep out water buffalo; inside shelves of boxed medicine, jars, swabs, depressors, Band-Aids, ointment, and MEDICO crates lined the walls. Locals waited in the front, holding chickens and eggs for payment. We played pinochle in the back room while the Navy doctor sat children on his knee, dripping vitamins on their tongues. Seven miles from China but we couldn't see red except on the boxes of Regent cigarettes. We scrubbed a tin of scalpels when the doctor carried-in a Pathet Lao soldier run over by a jeep; the doctor slit the man's pants and gave us his jacket. I ate clumped rice in the back room while wearing the soldier's jacket: the sleeves were short, the neck tight, but I did not want to take it off.

IV
Work

Work: Milling

Pestle-ground grain. Indian corn rubbed against a grater; meal collected on cloth. Sifted to mush, sifted to dust, beneath boots (a cousin from Missouri was found in the barn barefoot, heeling about, smelling like summer for days afterward). Grain sacks on the bottom level, formed like bloated stomachs, leaned against the back wall. More hemp than flax, woven by Vanessa, loom off the side of the kitchen. Her braided hair tucked behind thin ears. She liked the feel of cloth more than wheat, and she left the grain to her brother and sold mantas with stripes and bands (they were dyed with cochineal and globemallow). Rung as dry as the grain. All moisture sucked into steam, into clouds.

Work: Folding

That was the room where we folded clothes. Sweaters, pants, t-shirts.
Three tables formed in a triangle. I folded fast. Left hand over right. Fast,
but at an even clip, a consistent rhythm. We do this each night at 7, before
the moon falls, before it is time for sleep. I like doing this. I live for
texture. I need to feel in order to know. This is our world: we live in other
worlds, in streets and in schools, but we exist here, among these piles of
clothes, palms grazing buttons, wrists flattening collars. Night after night,
forearms torqued from repetition, noses stuffed from all this down, from all
this wool. Sometimes I can barely breathe. Like there is no air left in the
room that isn't contaminated by cloth. With each exhale my tongue trills
like it is painted in plaid. I fold until I am told to stop, but when I do stop I
step away, even if I am in half-motion. Even if that blouse is left splayed,
naked and untucked.

Work: Herding

Two-hundred fifty head of them. Black, almost blue, piebald calves grazing in crabgrass. Heads low. Riders in a line in front of them, forearms crossed on the heads of horses. Pistols snapped and hidden, but loaded. Last cowboy on the left, Pitch, caught sniffing around his wife's sister. Said he meant no harm. No man ever does. Women do, though. When they cheat they do so with purpose. Like Ms. Wilcox, headmistress of the farm, with her tired face but young hands. Her eyes alive. Stories about her in the guesthouse, pillowcases stamped with blush. They called the one calf who always left the fold Wilcox. She could somehow stray under clear sight; once they found her near a Norway maple flayed by heavy wind. Pitch remembered it well: he'd doctored the tree, mixed cement in a wheelbarrow and stuck the trunk. Wilcox was there even then, hands behind her back, next to her husband. One kept the other in line.

Work: Landscaping

Walk-behind, orange-decked lawnmowers in the county garage. Pushed
onto the truck's trailer, hitched with jumper cords. Once we hitched the
mower with twine, to see if it would stay: the drive was slow, our eyes
locked on the rear-view. Three hours spent at the Weights and Measures
building: mowing the back hill, slope muddied from Saturday rain. Sun
hidden behind clouds so the wind blew cold on bare arms and legs, the
same skin later pasted green and parts black from weed-whacking in the
parking lot, thrown gravel peppering the brick-backed building.
Abandoned. We sat in the bed of the truck and ate pork-roll sandwiches
with warm chocolate milk. Then we looked inside the building: rows of
scales with county seals. We couldn't see the dust but knew it coated every
inch.

Work: Sugaring

Kneel before the tree, pull the knife neck-level, right to left, back to right. Bark split: set the spile. Point it down. Sap drubs into the buckets (slow as the moon or a sick fox). Once filled the buckets are carried two at a time (Daniel's shoulders look like a yoke; his teeth look like a horse). Sap boiled thick, massaged with hands (so many hands, palms film-full, sticky even after soap). Cooled to a near-dust. Rubbed into fish, mixed with water (and afterward Daniel sits at the table, hat askew, heels of his hands stained like tanned leather--he is smiling, though he doesn't show his teeth. They are nearly gone, but certainly not from anything sweet).

Work: Logging

Billings bunkhouse: socks, boots, overalls, vests, flannels, and longjohns draped from strings. View from front window: field, banked tight. View from back window: horseshoe turn on Fairmont Bridge. More than one man has died on that route. No woman has yet died there. Half the boarders came from the northern farms, harvesters. Men who rode the binder at midnight, lanterns leading the way through wheat. They'd run a bar out of the basement of a shoe store but it was raided by the sheriff, who dumped the kegs in a gulley, beige froth pooling in the mud. More than one man sucked the dirty beer until it settled into the ground. Now they had moved on to the forest, dehorning trees, crotched trunks, double-bitted axes stuck in logs. They sometimes thought of the sheave-bound wheat, threshed the next morning. Or, rather, they thought of the dirty sweetness. The memory of a tongue.

Work: Farming

June. White-pink flowers open, cranberries picked from the bog with a scoop (months before the water, browned, hid vines reddened from cold). Cucumbers are grown in the greenhouse, hung from rafters. Farmer fell asleep at the kitchen table, coughing back snores. Breaths paused. Sounded like he was dead. On the stove a pot overflowed. Crisp gemelli flowed across linoleum, carried by the boiled water, pooled around his boots. Water in the house, water outside: storm continued through the night. Ended with a smack of humidity. Then came the bugs. Burned pine sawdust to kill the mosquitoes. Broomy, feather-winged carcasses lined the cement floor. His cousin, years ago, had developed an ammoniac spray that killed the bugs on contact but left the sprayer with a swollen throat. That was no good. No more bites, but no more breath, either.

Work: Guiding

Couples most often; rarely does a single person seek a controlled route.
Conrad, an orienteer, greets at the gate and steals the most athletic visitors.
The other guides wait behind, though they should have learned that lesson
a thousand times. Most people want to take the horses rather than go on
foot (beginners are too scared to be scared, content to be up higher than
normal). It is a soft cross over the creek. The meadows are marshy and
the connecting roads steeped with gravel. There is no easiest path. Men,
more than woman, ask to stop at the bathroom near the lookout. They
have a hell of a time getting off the horse, and once on the ground the grass
is new and their knees wide. They are loud in the bathroom: too much iced
tea at lunch, and the women stay on their horse, at first talking with the
guide, and then staring out into the trees. Wondering.

Work: Butchering

Everyone hopes for wind. North-west, south-east, any direction. On still days the smell is enough to turn even the tightest stomach. Blood in casks, hot under thick roofs. Fat taken to Hopewell. The rest of the pig is taken elsewhere. The planked-floors are soft from runoff; a dragged boot peels back splinter. The moisture that doesn't seep into the wood drains to Penn's Creek, which curls but never seems to cool (men in waders claim to feel the heat through the rubber). Those who want the slaughterhouse gone claim fish taken from the current (particularly carp) have a rusty taste. The owner, a first-generation Pole, said carp wasn't supposed to taste good. Certainly not as good as pig.

Work: Teaching

Asked to use writing in the mathematics classroom, he photocopied poems by Frost (his mind was associative, like a poet's, someone once said, so he thought poetry - Frost - Vermont - sugar - maple - bacon - omelet). He placed the copy on each student's desk (distributing handouts allowed him to better meter time than students passing the work down row) and they rolled eyes, said fuck, flipped over the paper. Most already had English that morning, participated in choral readings with Ms. Berryrose, intoning Edgeworth's *Belinda* over the whittling heater. Now, again, at 1:25? He rewrote the first line of "Out, Out" on the board, and then marked iambs, the only thing he remembered from his college poetics course. He reminded them that Weierstrass said that the complete mathematician must also be something of a poet. They asked who Weierstrass was; the teacher asked the same question about poetry. Nobody knew.

Work: Gardening

Hired last winter after the previous groundskeeper, a Swedish husbandman, retired to Georgia, an expanded ranch on the edge of a state park. Earned a certificate in horticulture from the state university and a license to operate backhoe from the county. Learned afterward the license wasn't even necessary. Garden was 50 by 50, tucked in the center of the property (owners were the Ladd sisters, runners of a defunct convalescence home, now convalescents themselves). Planted hop hornbeam in a weaving row, bark looked scarred but layered. Candytuft between rocks, red-lavender flowers fluttered even when air was still. Purple-flowered scabiosa. Always cut them at the stalk for when the Ladd sisters visited. Two weeks out of the year they returned home, slept in their old beds, ate at their old table, and sniffed the old flowers. They would wilt soon, but for those two weeks they bloomed.

Work: Fishing

Not work. Hours on the Susquehanna, in mid-afternoon, when most
people think walleye hide, when bass troll the bottom. Most people are
wrong about fishing. There is little to know. He went to an Orvis camp
when he was twelve and watched a seasonal park ranger model a fly cast
using a metronome. He took his sister's metronome from the baby grand in
the dining room and put it in his johnboat, floating in the farm pond.
There is no meter to a regular cast, though, only placement and pace.
Under willow branches, in pockets shadowed by pairs of evergreens. Some
afternoons are good. This one is great: seven trout taken with only
nightcrawlers and leaders. But he is lost in some thought, and close to
shore rock punctures the hull. Water soothes across fiberglass, giving the
trout new breath: they flap, blood electric. He stuffs the hole with a balled
sweater and the canoe lolls. He catches his breath though he hadn't
realized he'd lost it, the sliding sets of eyes watching.

V
Parishes

Holy Family

Built 1915.

Three black-necked sparrows burrowed in the eaves. Nest of thistle, crabgrass, root. A third-year brother, Alan, set a ladder on the north side of the church. The babies had flapped and flown, gone. The mother nestled in a willow on the south slope of the property. Alan had spoken to his own mother that morning and, after customary talk, had let his guard down during some first grade nostalgia (his teacher, a Mrs. Downey, had just died, her name second from last in the bulletin). He said he was going to the roof. His mother read verbatim from the farmer's almanac, warning equal parts rain and wind. He promised to wait until the weekend but knew his plans would not change. He knew a empty nest would soon be occupied and another band of sparrows would pilt droppings along the sidewalks, the handrail. Woods extended for miles on the north hill but the birds demanded to live here. Brother Alan settled the ladder and put on his gloves. Father Nolan stepped out from under the door, coffee in hand. He looked up at the clouds, then at Alan, and said we all take chances in life.

Oratory of Old St. Patrick

Built 1887.

Communal calisthenics. Father Antonio, a first-generation Galician, had published several treatises in Spain (*Rezando y Caminando*, *Dios de Accion*) and spoke of motion as the apex of existence. Though he was clear to explain away the heresy of Lucretius (he who said we are but containers for jiggling atoms), Antonio explained that we are doubly in motion, internal and external. Even sleep is not stasis. So why not move ourselves forward in our journey toward God? He organized Saturday morning trai hikes, moderate speed walks through county parks, military-like lines, staggered and narrow, of barely mobile septuagenarians and overanxious teens, who were in the process of composing their own scheme of body, for whom sex was still new or fear, a mystery. Not the mystery of mysteries. But still mysterious.

Blessed Sacrament

Built 1929.

A visiting deacon had smashed the hand of Father Gil in the door of a Bel Air that belonged to the mayor. The three, all alumni of St. Augustine, had gone to Don Pepe for lunch. Father Gil said their pulpo was steamed right, doused with salt that flickered on the white.

No broken bones but a good swelling, and the priest balled ice in his fist. When opened white marks pleated his skin. He could not fully perform mass so the junior priest of the next parish, St. Brigid, assisted, though the two did not see eye to eye. The latter's Spanish was stilted--one woman said he spoke as if he stood in an earthquake. But his homilies were focused and short. One concluded with an analogy to Cicero's dismembered hands. Father Gil appreciated the recognition but still felt slight, moving the limp limb behind his back during the Creed.

St. Jude

Built 1957.

The thrift shop opened in 1976. A widowed parishioner donated a basement of books (geologic texts, Victorian novels), clothes (moccasins, corduroys, dress shirts with faint sweat stains starched a temporary white), and croquet sets (her husband was a crafter of them). The shop was housed below the boiler room and was always hot and a bit wet; the first employee, Shelley Yates, claimed she could thumb a sheen of sweat off Graham Greene's face on the back row of book covers. Donations were accepted Monday through Thursday, noon to two, and a surprising number of damaged garments were attempted to be passed on, in addition to food gone sour. No food was even accepted. The croquet sets sat in the back of the store, severely underpriced, though dusted every few months. One deacon asked to borrow a set for the weekend (he was to attend a family reunion and his brother always insisted on volleyball, a game he'd lose and would likely result in injury) but Shelley said he should just buy it. But he said he only wanted to borrow. And that back and forth continued until both seemed to run out of words.

Mary, Queen of Angels

Built 1901

Perpetual adoration of the rosary: Monday nights, 6 to 7:30. Sacrament of penance: Saturday, 3 to 4:30. Bible study, 1 to 3. Pirogue sale, meeting of Irish-Canadian Catholics, debate between Knights of Columbus and Secular Franciscans, all booked at the same time: 5 to 7 pm, Wednesday. Patty Ann, parish secretary, triple-booked and blamed the act on the new parish register, a cross-hatch of green lines against white, dates arranged vertical, leaning to the left, numbers lost to her sight. Melanie Steinwitz arrived at 4:30, dough in tow, aluminum foil sheets stacked in the back of her husband's Wrangler. The president and vice president of the Irish-Canadian Catholics both arrived at 4:30. Last to arrive were the debaters, who'd spent the afternoon at the pub. It was decided that the discussion should be congenial, not bogged down by fact. So much was open to interpretation, and fancies, like faith, come and go.

Our Lady of Mercy

Built 1876.

Parish annex converted to a theatre: priest had studied Eugene O'Neill at Yale, performed in *The Great God Brown* before entering seminary. Eschewed passion plays, instead holding dialogues from the Byzantine poet Romanus. Two or three actors on the bare pine stage (just a thin varnish to keep the wood). Actors were plain-clothed, some in ties from work, high school students stopping-in after practice, pediatricians in olive sport coats. The point was to settle into the roles without pretense. Father Harris explained this through a discussion of Beckett's barebone production, *Ohio Impromptu*. One of the parish actors, a deputy county clerk, asked if it was necessary to speak in Latin. Harris crossed his arms and said the contrast was everything. Living bodies plus dead language equaled new emotions.

St. Ladislaus

Built 1813

Father North used to be the pastor of the Lutheran St. Luke's right down the street. When he became Catholic he brought his family with him: wife and two sons. Took the parishioners some time to get used to: they'd heard of such a thing, a married priest, but to see it in the flesh was another world. They laughed about it before mass, in the parish center, hands on crossed legs; during the mass, early in pews, initial prayers on kneelers; and then after mass, at tables in the hallway, raffle tickets and pledge cards in piles. But they kept their faces straight during interactions, shaking his hand with an even stroke, talking about the CYO team. Waiting. Waiting to see a muted argument with his wife in the parking lot. Wondering what it would look like for a priest to hold the hand of a woman.

Divine Providence

Built 1900. Burned 1980. Rebuilt 1983.

Father Holaday woke on the rectory floor, cheek and mouth on the green shag carpet, bare feet extending to the hardwood. Original cherry, deep varnished, so slick he could never wear socks. He had not been drinking. He never drank. He stood and watched flames cover the roof of the church. He thought it like a dream, got back into bed, and was awakened minutes later by Sister Regina. That alone was enough shock. The monsignor called them Sisters of the Snore, their nightly chokes and coughs kept them asleep through everything, even when a peeping tom pressed his bare stomach against a window. The church was burning, she said. So dream was not a dream. He wondered how it could have started. A fallen votive? Arson? Yet he could not even know why he'd slept on the ground. No answers to the small questions results in ignorance of the bigger concerns.

Sangre de Cristo

Built 1989

Three men in the farthest row on the left sneezed during the Intercessions. The sneezes were not concurrent, though they did punctuate the prayers in a such a manner that, during the offering of the gifts, Father Meier snuck a glance back to their area. He remembered their faces and would make it a point, during the exit procession, to offer an even more deliberate look in their direction. But they left after communion, each of them opting for the left row, the one with Deacon Perry, who paused before placing the Host on hand. Father Meier asked the cantor and she said she knew one of the men but he hadn't come to mass in years. And what is years, asked the priest? 20 years, the cantor said, and she was as sure of that statement as she was of the price of blackberries at the Mill Street Market (though she got that wrong). One of the men used to organize the carnival to benefit the school. He'd purchased a day liquor license, thinking the sales would bring money. They did. But they brought worse, and it all ended with a man passed out in the front pew, a missal open on his bare stomach. He said he was warm and the pages were cold. That kind of man, she said, could use some church.

Little Flower

Built 1822. Moved 1917.

Father Coldwell had a sore throat: allergies each May made worse by a weekend pilgrimage through Black Apple National Forest (years earlier a hiker had reported seeing the Virgin's face in a lightening-felled stump). Called neighboring parish, St. Joseph, and the parish secretary thought Coldwell was having a heart attack and called the police. A State Trooper was nearest to the scene and he found Coldwell in the living room, green tea stewing on the table, sugar cookies spread on a plate. Both men looked equally surprised. All parishes in the county were contacted but no priest was available: baptisms, inductions into the church, reformations, and more. Even the bishop's office was called, though a monsignor warned that it was ill-advised to contact the archbishop over such a local matter. So the priest only held one mass, at noon, and distributed a photocopy explaining the situation. He rested his voice during the Our Father: even a whisper would carry with the chorus.

Nuestra Senora de Guadalupe del Valle Pojoaque

Built 2001.

Washing of feet: twelve people lined behind the church. Three pieces of plywood, side by side, holes in the center of each for draining. Hose pulled out, faucet on. Khakis rolled to calves, dresses pressed against thighs. Socks tucked into boots, lined in the grass like children's backpacks. Father Regan in sandals, sleeves pulled back to his elbows. White towels on both his shoulders. This year there are three women. Father Regan knew he would have to answer someone, whether it was a side comment or a direct question: why the females? At first he would answer with a joke (what man wouldn't rather see the attractive feet of a woman than the knobby feet of a man)? He would wash feet, pull his hand along heels, dribble water along the tips of toes. And then he would claim permission from the Holy See. Direct permission? Permission is never direct. Not from God. Would all of us want to believe in so simple a relationship?

Resurrection

Built 1981.

St. Gabriel, pray for us. St. Mark, pray for us. All you holy Innocents, pray for us.

Pray for the vertical crack along the east wall; once hairline, now webbed, threading between the fifth and sixth stations of the cross.

The stations under which Father Donovan, a Franciscan from St. Louis, plays the punished Christ each Good Friday.

Father Donovan played football for the University of Missouri. Only for one season. He was a cornerback, and each morning went alone into the mess hall for a bagel with lox. It didn't matter what time he'd gone to bed the previous night, he would be there each morning at 5, before the cafeteria workers stepped out of the maroon van into the cold.

His father had told him such structure was necessary, like bones for muscle.

He thought his father said that. But when he leaned in-between the pews on those Fridays, the cross on his left shoulder, he wondered if that was true. About his father, about other things.

What is truth?

About the Author

Nick Ripatrazone earned his undergraduate degree from Susquehanna University and graduate degrees from Rutgers University, where he has taught courses on sport literature and contemporary American fiction. He has also taught public-school English since 2004. His writing has appeared in *Esquire, The Kenyon Review, West Branch, The Mississippi Review, Caketrain, The Saint Ann's Review, Abjective, Annalemma, The Collagist, SmokeLong Quarterly, Sou'wester* and *Beloit Fiction Journal*. He lives with his wife in northern New Jersey.

CPSIA information can be obtained at www.ICGtesting.com

228349LV00005B/84/P

9 780982 630969